For Mom & Dad,
whose kisses I caught
&
Connor, Eden, and Brynn,
who catch mine.
—A. G.

To Peter. You are the wind in the sails of my dreams.
—M. V. L.

A FEIWEL AND FRIENDS BOOK
An Imprint of Macmillan

Feiwel and Friends books may be purchased for business or promotional use.
For information on bulk purchases, please contact the Macmillan Corporate and Premium
Sales Department at (800) 221-7945 x5442 or by e-mail at specialmarkets@macmillan.com.

Library of Congress Cataloging-in-Publication Data Available

ISBN: 978-0-312-37647-5

The artwork was created with Adobe Illustrator.

Book design by Maria van Lieshout and April Ward
Display type created by Maria van Lieshout

Feiwel and Friends logo designed by Filomena Tuosto

First Edition: 2013

10 9 8 7 6 5 4 3 2 1

mackids.com

CATCHING KISSES

AMY GIBSON

illustrated by

MARIA VAN LIESHOUT

FEIWEL AND FRIENDS NEW YORK

At any given moment,
someone,
somewhere,
is blowing a kiss.

And somewhere, someone is catching it.

Kisses are sailing

PUBLIC
MARKET

FISH

FRUIT

FLOWERS

from porches and bus stops,
from windows and doors.

Like **thumbprints** and **snowflakes**,

no two are the same.

They smell of **ginger** and **cinnamon**,
tortillas and **oatmeal**,
fresh bread
and **hot chocolate**.

Some are **velvet**
as **peach fuzz**.

Some **tickle** like
whiskers.

Everyday, everywhere,
kisses are **flying**.

They're **invisible**,
but **real** as the
wind in your face.

They **zig!**
They **zag!**

through **taxis**

and **buses**

and streams
of bicycles.

eat
delicious

Come
fly the
friendly
skies

BEST
LOVE
STORY

Coffee&Bagels

TAXI

In rain or snow
or sleet or hail,

in any weather,
they make it through.

CAUTION
SLIPPERY
WHEN WET

Some SMACK!
like bubblegum.

Some whisper
like butterflies.

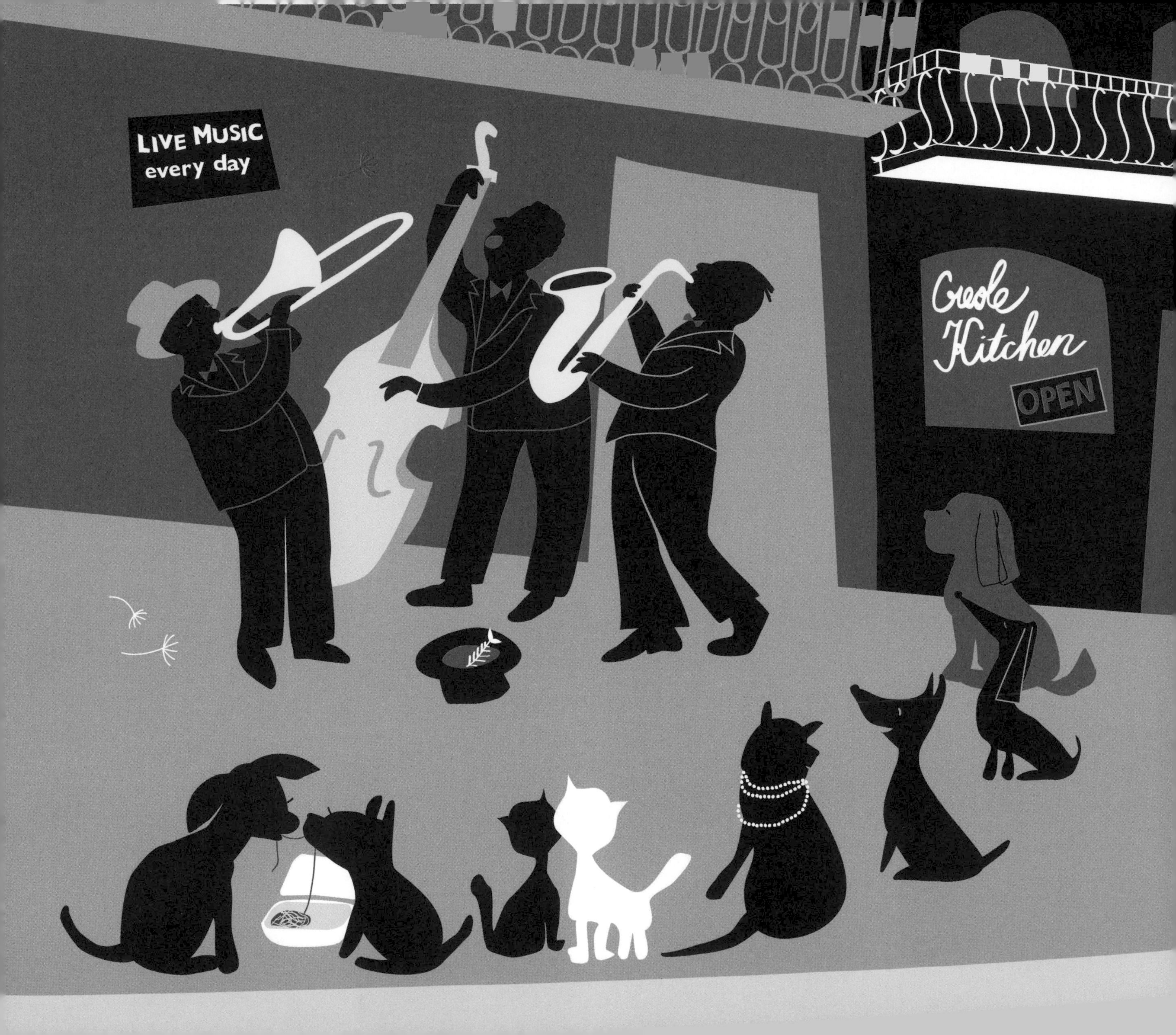
LIVE MUSIC
every day
Creole
Kitchen
OPEN

Kisses go with you
wherever,

whatever the day brings.

You can **hide** them
in your **pocket**.

You can **tuck** them
in your **book**.

You can **keep** them
like a **secret**

or fly them
like a **kite**.

Kisses are **powerful**.

No **wall** can
hold them back.

No **fence** can
keep them out.

They're soft as lamb's wool,
but strong as steel.

They're not afraid of **tears.**

And once a kiss is given,
anytime,
anywhere,

it can **never** be taken away.

It's yours.

DREAM

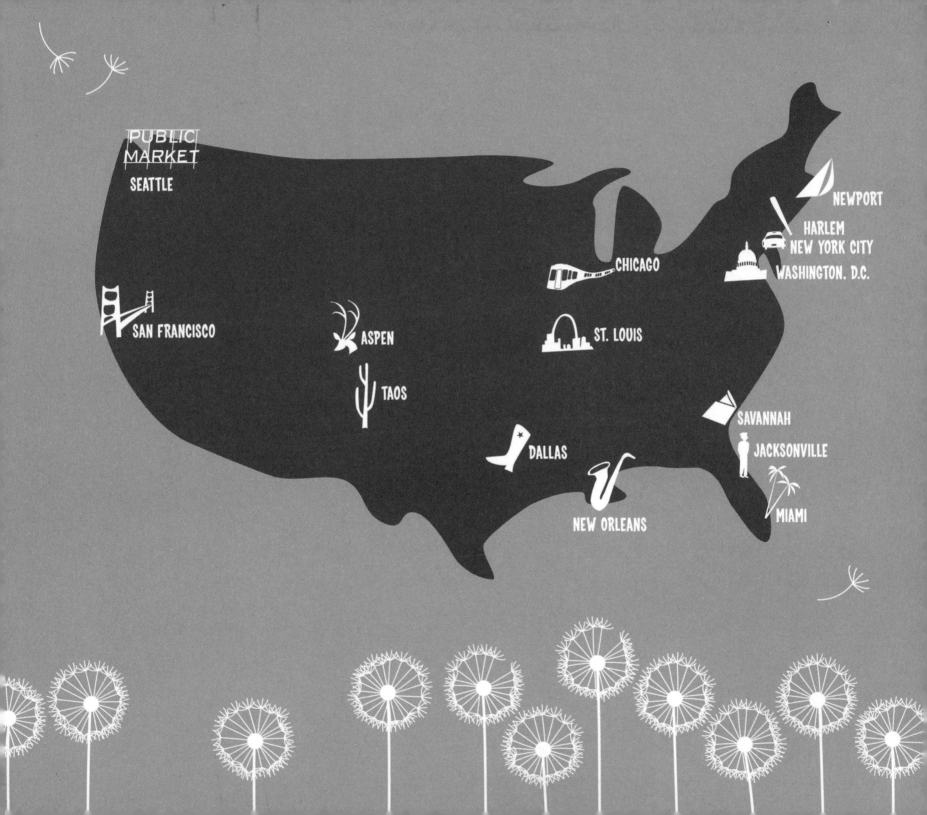